This edition published by Parragon Books Ltd in 2016

Parragon Books Ltd
Chartist House
15–17 Trim Street
Bath BA1 1HA, UK
www.parragon.com

ISBN 978-1-4748-4463-5

Printed in China

Disney · PIXAR

FINDING DORY

Parragon

Bath • New York • Cologne • Melbourne • Delhi
Hong Kong • Shenzhen • Singapore

Dory was a little blue tang who lived with her parents. From a very young age, Dory had trouble remembering things.

"Hi, I'm Dory," she would say, and then she would explain that she had short-term memory loss.

Dory's mum and dad did everything they could to stop her from getting lost. But one day, Dory couldn't find her way back home!

Dory just kept on swimming and swimming, getting farther and farther away from her home.

Time passed and Dory grew up, but she still asked every fish she met if they had seen her parents. None of them had.

"Hi, I've lost my family," Dory would say. "Can you help me?"

"Where did you see them last?" the fish would ask.

"Well ... uh. Funny story, but, uh ... I forgot."

Poor Dory had forgotten where she came from.

One day while Dory was swimming along, she swam head first into a clownfish, who was yelling something about his son, Nemo!

"They took him away!" the clownfish cried.

Kind-hearted Dory helped the clownfish, whose name was Marlin, search for his missing son.

One year later, long after Nemo was found, the three friends still lived together on the coral reef. They had a happy and colourful home, and had lots of fun together.

But one day, Dory got swept away in a strong current caused by a group of migrating stingrays. Her world spun around her and then faded to black.

While she was knocked out, Dory muttered something under her breath: "The Jewel of Morro Bay, California."

She woke up with a flood of memories in her head. She had remembered her parents and her home – she was from California!

Dory asked Marlin and Nemo to travel across the ocean with her to find her parents. They hitched a ride to California with their old friend, Crush the turtle, and soon arrived in Morro Bay, ready to start their search.

Just then, Dory was scooped up by a human and carried away in a boat! There was nothing Marlin and Nemo could do.

A voice came over a loudspeaker in the distance: "Welcome to the Marine Life Institute, where we believe in Rescue, Rehabilitation and Release."

The next thing Dory knew, she had a tag clipped to her fin and was dropped into a tank. Suddenly, an octopus appeared. He had one tentacle missing – he was a 'septopus'! He reached one of his long tentacles towards Dory. "Name's Hank," he said.

Hank explained that Dory was in Quarantine, and the tag on her fin was a transport tag – it meant she was going to be taken to an aquarium in Cleveland.

"Cleveland!" gasped Dory. "No, I can't go to the Cleveland! I have to get to the Jewel of Morro Bay, California...."

"That's this place," said Hank. "The Marine Life Institute. The JEWEL of Morro Bay, California. You're here."

Hank said he would help Dory search for her parents if she gave him her transport tag. He liked the idea of living in a nice, safe tank in Cleveland – he didn't want to be sent back to the ocean. Dory agreed to the deal, so Hank scooped her up into a coffee pot full of water and they set off.

Dory and Hank found a map of the Institute and tried to decide where to look. A member of staff appeared and Hank hid, but Dory read the word on the staff member's bucket – it said 'DESTINY'. Suddenly, Dory felt it was very important that she get into that bucket – so she did! Hank followed as fast as he could as Dory was carried away.

Moments later, Dory was tipped into a large pool, which was home to a whale shark called Destiny. The two got talking and Destiny realized that she had known Dory when they were young! Dory had lived in the Open Ocean exhibit next door and they used to talk to each other through the pipes. Destiny told Dory how to get to the Open Ocean exhibit by swimming through the pipes, but Dory was afraid she would get lost.

Suddenly, another memory flashed into Dory's mind – her dad used to tell her that there was *always* another way....

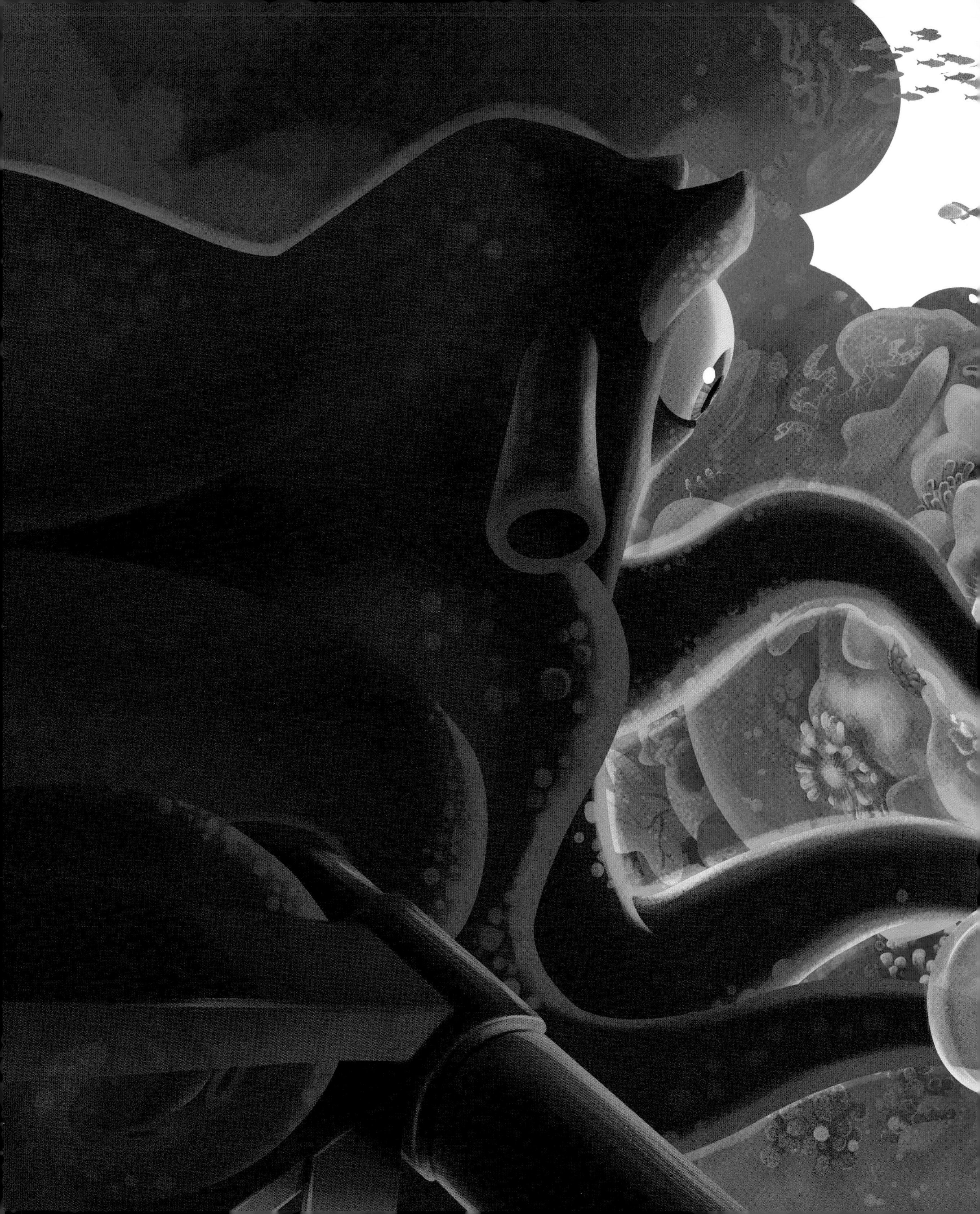

Dory spotted some pushchairs on the side of Destiny's pool.
"There!" said Dory. "We're gonna hijack one of those."
Dory jumped into a small cup of water on the tray of one of the pushchairs, and Hank sneakily pushed her across the Marine Life Institute.

They reached the Open Ocean exhibit and Dory handed Hank her tag. He had done his part.

"They're actually down there, aren't they?" Dory said, talking about her parents. "I hope I can find them."

"Knowing you," said Hank,"I'm liking your chances. Now go get your family."

With that, he gently dropped Dory into the water.

Dory swam down through the clear, cool tank. At the bottom, she saw a trail of shells and followed it. She suddenly remembered seeing the same trail when she was a child.

Dory gasped – this was her home! Her parents had made the shell path to guide her back whenever she got lost.

Just then, Dory noticed an entrance to a pipe. She remembered that her parents had warned her not to go near it, as the strong current it caused would carry her away. Young Dory had forgotten and been sucked into the pipe!

"It was my fault," Dory whispered. "My parents ... I lost them."

Dory swam in circles, not sure what to do next! A friendly crab spoke to her and explained that all the blue tangs had been taken to Quarantine, ready to be shipped to the aquarium in Cleveland. Dory couldn't believe it!

The only way back to Quarantine was through the pipes, so Dory nervously swam in ... and was soon lost.

But suddenly, two shapes emerged from the darkness. Marlin and Nemo had found her! They had met a bird called Becky who carried them in a bucket into the Institute to search for Dory.

Dory was thrilled! She explained everything, and the three of them found the way together.

When Marlin, Nemo and Dory reached Quarantine, the tank of blue tangs was about to be loaded on to the truck to Cleveland!

Luckily, Hank was there. He lifted Dory and her friends into a coffee pot and put them into the tank.

The other blue tangs recognized Dory, but they had sad news … Dory's parents had been sent to Quarantine years ago, and nobody knew what had happened to them.

Dory was heartbroken. She drifted slowly into the waiting coffee pot as Hank scooped it up and out of the tank.

"Where's everybody else?" asked Hank.

Marlin and Nemo were still inside the tank!

Just then, someone grabbed Hank. The coffee pot fell to the floor and shattered. Dory spilled into a drain, which took her back into the ocean.

Once again, she was alone.

Dory swam through the water out in the bay, wondering what she should do. Then something caught her eye – it was a shell trail. Dory liked shells, so she followed the trail.

Suddenly, two blue tangs appeared. Dory gasped. Her parents!

Dory's parents had been creating shell pathways all this time, in the hope that Dory would see them and remember.

“It’s you! It’s really you!” cried Dory as she burst into tears.

“Oh, honey, you found us,” said Dory’s mum. “And you know why you found us? Because you remembered. You remembered in your own amazing Dory way.”

Dory was so happy, but she hadn’t forgotten her other family, Marlin and Nemo. She had to save them!

With help from Destiny – who had leaped over the Institute wall and into the ocean – and some other new friends, Dory caught up with the truck that was carrying Marlin and Nemo and forced it to stop on a bridge. Destiny used her tail to flip Dory up and then Hank, who had sneaked on board the truck earlier, helped her into the tank with her friends.

Nemo was touched to see Dory. "Dory! You came back!"

Dory smiled. "Of course. I couldn't leave my family."

Marlin called for Becky the bird to come and get them. Becky arrived, but only scooped up Marlin and Nemo. She left Dory behind!

Marlin, Nemo and Dory's parents watched as the driver closed the truck doors and drove away. Dory and Hank were trapped!

But, back on the truck, Hank slid through a vent in the roof and down on to the windscreen. The shocked driver pulled over and jumped out. Hank slid inside, locked the doors and started to drive!

"Hank," said Dory, "I'm going to ask you to do something crazy."

Dory's family watched in amazement as Hank drove the truck straight off the bridge – and into the ocean! The doors flew open and all the fish spilled out into the sea. They were free!

Dory returned to life on the reef. Her whole blue tang family and all her new friends joined her. She was happier than she had ever been!

But Marlin was nervous that Dory would get lost again and often followed her. One day, Marlin caught up with Dory and they bobbed in the water at the edge of the reef, gazing out into the blue.

"Wow. It really is quite a view," said Marlin.

"Yup," replied Dory, "unforgettable."